KEROPPI™

The Best Friends Book
created by SANRIO

SCHOLASTIC INC.

New York   Toronto   London   Auckland   Sydney

ISBN 0-590-55823-4

12 11 10 9 8 7 6 5 4 3   8 9/9 0 1 2/0

Printed in the U.S.A.   40

First Scholastic printing, April 1998

Hi! I'm Keroppi! This is my best friend, Den Den. I love having a best friend! Den Den knows everything about me. He knows what makes me laugh — and what makes me cry. He knows what songs are music to my ears — and what songs make me want to cover my ears. Den Den even knows some things about me that no one else does.

In this book, you and your very own best friend can keep a diary to record all of those special memories and facts about each other.

Later on in the book I'll show you how to have a best friends' party, and even how to write to each other in a best friends' secret code. There's a lot of other stuff in this book for you and your best friend to do. So what are you waiting for? Grab your best friend and hop to it!

On the bottom of every page of this book, you'll find a word in a secret code. Keep track of the words to get a special message from me to you! Turn to page 36 to learn how to crack the code.

KEROPPI'S SECRET CODE

Picture-Perfect

I love getting my picture taken! This photo of Den Den and me is one of my favorites.

Do you have a favorite photo of you and your best friend? Paste it here.

PASTE PHOTO OF YOU AND YOUR BEST FRIEND HERE

KEROPPI'S SECRET CODE

We're Best Friends

My birthday is July 10. When's yours? When's your best friend's? Write down your birthday and some other important stuff here.

ME	MY BEST FRIEND
Name:_____	Name:_____
Address:_____	Address:_____
_____	_____
Phone Number:_____	Phone Number:_____
Birthday:_____	Birthday:_____
Age:_____	Age:_____

FaMiLy FUN

I live on Donut Pond with my mom and dad. My dad's a doctor. He wants me to follow in his flippers someday, but I think I'm more like my mom. She has a really great sense of humor. But enough about me. Who are the people in your families?

I remember when he was just a little tadpole!

ME	MY BEST FRIEND
Family members	Family members
1. _____	1. _____
2. _____	2. _____
3. _____	3. _____
Pets	Pets
1. _____	1. _____
2. _____	2. _____

KEROPPI'S SECRET CODE

You and Me

I like Den Den because he's smart, loyal, and can tell the future! Den Den says he likes me because I'm adventurous, kind, and funny. What are the three words that describe your best friend?

Keroppi's the coolest!

Den-Den's the best friend around!

The three words that describe my best friend are . . .

ME	MY BEST FRIEND
1. _____	1. _____
2. _____	2. _____
3. _____	3. _____

KEROPPI'S SECRET CODE

Hanging Out

Den Den and I hang out together a lot. Sometimes we go into town or to the movies. Other times we go to our clubhouse in the middle of Donut Pond and play. What do you and your best friend do when you hang out? Where do you go?

ME	MY BEST FRIEND

My favorite place to hang out is . . .

_____   _____

I love to hang out with . . .

_____   _____

My least favorite place to hang out is . . .

_____   _____

KEROPPI'S SECRET CODE

8

COOL TUNES

I'm in a band! We're called Keroppi and the Cattails. I sing and play lead guitar. My friend Soak is on horn. Den Den is our drummer. No wonder we're not famous anywhere outside of Donut Pond. (Den Den has a hard time holding the drumsticks.)

ME	MY BEST FRIEND

The best song I've heard this year is . . .

_____ _____

My favorite singer or group is . . .

_____ _____

If I were in a band, I'd call it . . .

_____ _____

If I could play any instrument, it would be . . .

_____ _____

KEROPPI'S SECRET CODE

Favorite Flicks

I love to go to the movies to escape. Comedies are my favorite, but every once in a while I like to go see a thriller. My friend Crabby likes musicals. He likes to snap his claws along with the songs.

That's because I can't sing!

ME	MY BEST FRIEND

My favorite movie is . . .

_____   _____

My favorite movie star is . . .

_____   _____

When I'm at the movies, I like to snack on . . .

_____   _____

KEROPPI'S SECRET CODE

10

TV Time

On rainy days my friends and I like to watch TV
at my place. We can never agree on what to watch!
I wish I could declare myself King of
Donut Pond so everyone
would have to watch
my favorite show.

ME	MY BEST FRIEND

The channel I watch most is . . .

_____   _____

The TV show I never miss is . . .

_____   _____

My favorite TV star is . . .

_____   _____

KEROPPI'S SECRET CODE

🌲 ☀ 🍃 🍃 ☀ 🐟 ☀

_ _ _ _ _ _ _

Sweet Stuff

When I get a sweet tooth, I always reach for ice cream. It doesn't matter what flavor — vanilla, chocolate, raspberry — I love them all!

ME	MY BEST FRIEND

When I want something sweet, I grab . . .

_____

My favorite ice cream flavor is . . .

_____

The best dessert I know how to make is . . .

_____

KEROPPI'S SECRET CODE

PaSS tHe PeaS, PLeaSe

A growing frog like me can't live on ice cream all the time. Some of my other favorite foods are actually good for me. Mom makes sure I eat my veggies at dinnertime, but fruit is my all-time favorite. Maybe it's because it comes in cool colors!

ME   MY BEST FRIEND

My favorite fruit is . . .

_____   _____

My favorite food of all time is . . .

_____   _____

The food that makes my stomach turn is . . .

_____   _____

KERoPPI'S SECRET CoDE

Hot Stuff

When summer turns up the heat I love to swim all day long. My friend Soak is a great underwater swimmer. He likes to sneak up on me at the pond and scare me by jumping up out of the water. I don't really mind. I can always splash him back!

ME	MY BEST FRIEND

My favorite summer activity is . . .

_____   _____

The best way to stay cool in summer is to . . .

_____   _____

The best thing about summer is . . .

_____   _____

Keroppi's Secret Code

COLD STUFF

Brrr! Sometimes I miss the summer sun when freezing winter comes, but that's OK, because winter can be fun, too. My friends and I like to ski and sled on Donut Pond.

Winter is snow cool!

ME

MY BEST FRIEND

My favorite winter activity is . . .

_____

The best way to stay warm in winter is to . . .

_____

The thing I like best about winter is . . .

_____

KEROPPI'S SECRET CODE

SCHOOL'S COOL!

My friend Newton is a great inventor. His favorite school subject is science. I like to learn about geography because I love to travel around the world. And of course I love recess, because then I can play with my friends!

I couldn't invent a friend better than you!

ME

MY BEST FRIEND

My favorite subject is . . .

_____ _____

My favorite teacher is . . .

_____ _____

The best day of school is always . . .

_____ _____

KEROPPI'S SECRET CODE

Cover to Cover

There's nothing I like better than curling up on my lily pad with a good book. When I read about adventurous heroes like Robin Hood, I feel like I'm traveling through time. It's like going on vacation without leaving home.

| ME | MY BEST FRIEND |

The last book I read was . . .

_____

My favorite book of all time is . . .

_____

My favorite author is . . .

_____

KEROPPI'S SECRET CODE

CHores! CHores! CHores!

I like to go places with my friends, but I can't go far if my pockets are empty. To earn money, I do chores for my mom and dad. I paint, collect firewood, or fix things around the house.

Sometimes Den Den helps me. That makes it a lot more fun. Does your best friend ever help you with your chores?

ME	MY BEST FRIEND

Some of the chores I do are . . .

_____   _____

The chore I like best is . . .

_____   _____

The chore I like least is . . .

Dog   Poop
_____

KEROPPI'S SECRET CODE

I Love to Shop

I love to go clothes shopping with Keroleen. She calls herself a "professional shopper." She can always pick out the perfect shirt for me. And when my birthday is near, she always picks out the perfect present for me. (And I can pick out the perfect one for her, too!)

| ME | MY BEST FRIEND |

My favorite piece of clothing is . . .

_____   _____

My favorite place to shop is . . .

_____   _____

The thing I would love to buy is . . .

_____   _____

KEROPPI'S SECRET CODE

Go, Team, Go!

Den Den and I joined the baseball team together. I'm great at hitting home runs. Den Den likes pitching. He's very dedicated to his sport. It's not easy for him to throw the ball with his mouth!

I may not have a fastball, but you should see my curveball!

ME	MY BEST FRIEND

The sport I am best at is . . .

So _____   _____

My favorite sports team is . . .

_____   _____

The sports star I would most like to meet is . . .

_____   _____

KEROPPI'S SECRET CODE

TiMe Out

Living in Donut Pond is great, but it's nice to take a break once in a while. I love to travel to exotic beaches all over the world. Once my friends and I all went on vacation together. It was a lot of fun — until we got home and noticed that my green skin was bright red with a sunburn!

| ME | MY BEST FRIEND |

On my favorite vacation, I went to . . .

FLORDA _____

The best souvenir I ever got was . . .

_____   _____

If I could go anywhere in the world, I'd visit . . .

_____   _____

KEROPPI'S SECRET CODE

Wild About Animals

I think animals are fascinating! After all, my best friend is a snail. But I guess my favorite animal of all time is a dragonfly. They can fly from place to place really fast,

and their bodies are rainbow-colored. That's one bug that doesn't bug me at all!

ME	MY BEST FRIEND

My favorite animal is . . .

Frogs

If I could have any animal in the world as a pet, I'd pick . . .

The animal that is most like me is . . .

KEROPPI'S SECRET CODE

Party Time!

I like all kinds of parties — big and small. Every weekend
I have a small sleepover in the clubhouse with my friends.
On birthdays we have big parties. The best party I ever
went to was my best friend Den Den's birthday party.
All our friends were there — Keroleen, Soak, Junk, and
Newton. We all had a blast! What's your favorite
kind of party?

For me?
You shouldn't
have!

ME

MY BEST FRIEND

My favorite kind of party is . . .

_____

The best party I've ever been to was . . .

_____

Things I like to do at parties are . . .

_____

KEROPPI'S SECRET CODE

Doing Things

Junk and I like doing many things together, like going swimming, telling jokes, and especially fishing. It's easy for us to do things together because we both like the same stuff — most of the time, that is! Check off the things you and your best friend like to do together.

___Go Swimming

___Picnic

___Play Board Games

___Tell Secrets

___Watch TV

___Tell Jokes

___Cook

___Share a Book

KEROPPI'S SECRET CODE

___Eat Ice Cream   ___Go to the Library

___Roller-skate   ___Go Shopping

___Exchange Presents   ___Go to the Amusement Park

___Do Homework   ___Go Camping

___Make Promises   ___Go to Birthday Parties

___Go on Trips   ___Go to Sporting Events

___Ride Bicycles   ___Go to the Aquarium

___Go to the Movies   ___Go for Walks/Runs

___Go to the Zoo   ___Go Out to Dinner

___Go to the Pizza Parlor   ___ Other _____

KEROPPI'S SECRET CODE

Nighty Night

Going to school, playing in a band, and traveling around the world can make you pretty tired. There's a trick I use when I can't fall asleep. I don't count sheep — I count fish! That puts me to sleep in no time.

ME	MY BEST FRIEND

The latest I ever stayed up was . . .

ALL NIGHT

In the best dream I ever had, I . . .

In the scariest nightmare I ever had, I . . .

KEROPPI'S SECRET CODE

Color Me Green

I like green because it's the color of trees, grass — and me! Den Den likes blue the best because it's the color of his shell and the color of the sky. Newton mixed our favorite colors together for us and got turquoise. What color do you get when you and your best friend mix your favorite colors? Try it and see!

My shell is blue, but I don't feel blue!

ME	MY BEST FRIEND

My favorite color is . . .

LIGHT GREEN

The best thing I ever made in art class was . . .

If I could paint my room any color, I'd paint it . . .

WALL PAPER WITH

FROGS, LIZARDS,
Turtles KEROPPI'S SECRET CODE

SHaKeS aND SHiVerS

My friend Junk looks pretty tough, doesn't he? He's the strongest guy in Donut Pond. Can you believe he is afraid of the dark? That's OK. Everyone is afraid of something — even me! I can *never* keep my eyes open during a scary movie.

I can't help it. I get really scared in the dark!

ME	MY BEST FRIEND

The thing that scares me most is . . .

_____   _____

The scariest book I ever read was . . .

_____   _____

The scariest movie I ever saw was . . .

_____   _____

KEROPPI'S SECRET CODE

That's So Embarrassing!

One morning I was so late for school that I ran out of the house at top speed — and got to class before I realized I was in my pajamas! How embarrassing! Everyone laughed. Luckily, the teacher let me go home and change. I hope nothing like that ever happens again!

ME	MY BEST FRIEND

The most embarrassing thing that ever happened to me was when . . .

_____   _____

It made me feel . . .

_____   _____

Keroppi's Secret Code

_____

Secret Crush

Isn't Keroleen the cutest? Den Den is the only one who knows I have a secret crush on her — at least I *think* he's the only one. Den Den says that the way I act around Keroleen, everybody in Donut Pond must know about it!

| ME | MY BEST FRIEND |

The person I have a secret crush on is . . .

_____   _____

If my crush ever found out, I'd feel . . .

~~Glad~~ Dumb   _____

The famous person I'd most like to go on a date with is . . .

_____   _____

OH, NO! / OH, YES!

The worst day of my life was the day that all my friends forgot about my birthday. But the best day of my life was the very next day, when they made it up to me with a big party! Friends are the best, aren't they?

ME	MY BEST FRIEND

The worst thing that ever happened to me was . . .

_____

The best thing that ever happened to me was . . .

_____

Sorry!

Sometimes I'll say something to a friend that will hurt his feelings. We make up by talking out our problem and saying we're sorry. Sometimes Den Den and I become even closer after a fight because we learn new things about each other after talking. Have you ever hurt your friend's feelings?

ME	MY BEST FRIEND

What hurts me the most is . . .

My Parents Broke
Up

My best friend and I got into a fight because . . .

We made up by . . .

We learned that . . .

KEROPPI'S SECRET CODE

32

Friends Forever

I'm so lucky that Den Den is my best friend! When I'm happy, he's happy for me. And when life gets me down, he's there to cheer me up. We're best friends, and no matter what happens, we'll be friends forever!

ME	MY BEST FRIEND

The thing I like most about my best friend is . . .

S_{HE} R_{ESPE}TCS
E_{VERY}ONE

I had the most fun with my best friend when we . . .

_____

The nicest thing my best friend ever did for me was . . .

_____

Best Friends, Best Secrets

Den Den and I have fun playing with all of our friends at Donut Pond. But sometimes we share secrets that are just between us (like my secret crush on Keroleen). Den Den is the best. He never tells anyone my secrets, and I never tell anyone his.

There are many ways to have fun with secrets. I'll tell you all about them on these next pages. Den Den and I decided it wouldn't be any fun to keep these great ideas a secret. Sometimes, secrets are best when you share them with a friend!

Shhh!
It's a secret!

KEROPPI'S SECRET CODE

CHOOSE YOUR SECRET NAMES

Den Den and I picked secret names that we call each other. Secret names come in handy when you're writing each other notes, or talking to each other on the phone. If other people happen to read your note, they won't know who wrote it or whom it's to!

You can pick any name in the world for your secret name. Maybe there's a name you've always wanted. If you don't have any ideas, try thinking of your favorite movie star, your favorite color, or even your favorite animal.

What? You want to know what *my* secret name is? Sorry, but I can't tell you. Then it wouldn't be a secret!

Me	My Best Friend

My secret name is . . .

_____   _____

Learn My Secret Code

Sometimes I wonder what it would be like to be a secret agent. I'd have cool tools, like a telephone hidden in my watch and a pen that writes in invisible ink.

Secret agents aren't the only ones who can use secret codes. Best friends can use them, too. You and your best friend can send each other messages that no one else can read.

Here is a special secret code that Den Den and I made up. You can use it, too. Each picture stands for the letter of the alphabet below it.

My name, Keroppi, looks like this in secret code:

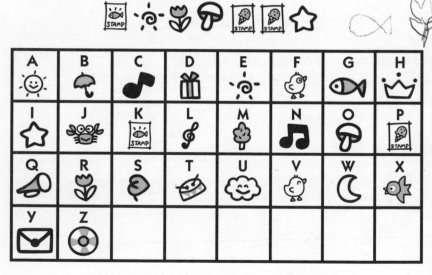

If you look carefully at the bottom of each page of this book, you'll see a word written in my secret code. Copy down the code in order to find out a super-secret message from me to you!

How to Send Secret Messages

You can use my secret code to send messages in all kinds of ways. There's only one way you shouldn't try — don't send each other messages in class! Den Den and I got caught passing notes in class once. We had to stay after school for a whole week.

Instead, try these other fun ways to send your secret messages:

- Send your messages through the mail. It may seem like a silly thing to do if you and your best friend see each other every day, but getting a letter in the mail is really special. Just make sure you *don't* use the secret code to write your friend's address on the envelope! Unless there's a secret agent working at your post office, he probably won't know whom to deliver the letter to.

I hide secret messages inside a tree stump.

KEROPPI'S SECRET CODE

F R I E N D

- Send your message in a sweet surprise. Fold up your message into a long, thin rectangle and slip it into the outer wrapper of a candy bar. Then give the candy bar to your friend at lunch.

- Slip the message into your friend's locker at school.

- Slip your message inside the pages of a book — say between pages 34 and 35. Then give the book to your friend, and say something like, "I thought you'd like to read this book. Something really exciting happens on page 34." When your friend turns to the page, she'll find the note.

Make Your OWN Secret Code

After you've practiced using my secret code, you and your best friend can make up a code of your very own. It's easy. Just remember that each letter must have its own special symbol to represent it. You can use pictures, like I did, or come up with some other way.

KEROPPI'S SECRET CODE

Here are some popular codes you can use:

- The number code. Give each letter a number, like A=1, B=2, etc.

- The backwards alphabet. A=Z, B=Y, C=X, etc. Use this space to write in your very own secret code:

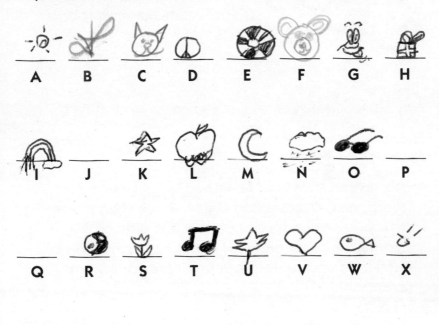

A B C D E F G H

I J K L M N O P

Q R S T U V W X

Y Z

KEROPPI'S SECRET CODE

Make a Best Friends' Scrapbook

I'll never forget the time Den Den and I won the Donut Pond three-legged race. I can't forget — I've got a photo of it with the first-place ribbon glued into our Best Friends' Scrapbook. You and your best friend can make a scrapbook, too. That way you'll never forget the good times you have together.

Step One: The Book

There are many things you can use as your scrapbook. Here are some ideas:

- Use several sheets of construction paper or poster board, all cut to the same size. Stack the papers in a neat pile. Punch three holes in one side of the papers. Thread a piece of yarn or ribbon through each hole and tie it into a bow. Presto! Instant scrapbook!

Keroppi's Secret Code

- Use a notebook. A three-ring binder is great because you can always add more pages.

- Use a photo album. The albums with paper pages work well, and so do the ones with the magnetic pages.

- Buy a blank scrapbook at an arts and crafts store.

Step TWo: Decorate the Cover

Once you've got a book, decorate the cover of your Best Friends' Scrapbook. Use crayons, markers, paint, glitter, ribbons, and scraps of paper to jazz it up. Den Den and I pasted a photo of the two of us together on the cover of our scrapbook.

KEROPPI'S SECRET CODE

Step Three: Add the Memories

A scrapbook is a place to put all the things that remind you and your best friend of the good times you've had. Here are some things to put in a scrapbook:

- Photos of you and your best friend

- Notes, letters, and postcards you write to each other

- Ticket stubs from movies you've seen together

- Programs and flyers from school events

- Pictures cut out from magazines of your favorite actors, animals, singers, foods — your favorite anything!

Before you start pasting, think about how you want to arrange your memories. Do you want a crazy mix of pictures? Or do you want to organize your pages into categories, like School, Parties, and Vacations? It's up to you — it's your scrapbook.

As you paste down your pictures and mementos, you can decorate your scrapbook pages with stickers, rubber stamps, or designs you and your best friend draw together.

Don't Worry iF you FiLL up your First Scrapbook.
You can aLWayS Make More!

KEROPPI'S SECRET CODE

Take the Best Friends Quiz

By now you should know all there is to know about your best friend. But to be sure, you should take my Best Friends Quiz!

Fill in the answers to the quiz questions on these pages first. Then let your best friend take the quiz on pages 45–46. When you're both done, you can check each other's answers. Then turn to page 47 to find out how you score as a best friend.

How Well Do I Know My Best Friend?

1. My best friend's birthday is _____ .

2. Circle the number of brothers and sisters your best friend has:
   a. 0   b. 1   c. 2   d. 3   e. 4   f. 5 or more

3. My best friend's favorite movie of all time is

   _____ .

4. My best friend's favorite movie star is

   _____ .

5. My best friend's favorite TV show is

   _____ .

6. My best friend's favorite music group is
   HANSON BROTHERS _____ .

KEROPPI'S SECRET CODE

7. The one food I should never serve to my best friend is <u>BEANS</u>.

8. My best friend's favorite ice cream flavor is

_____.

9. My best friend's favorite subject in school is

_____.

10. My best friend's hobby is

_____.

11. My best friend's favorite sports team is

_____.

12. The thing my best friend likes to shop for most is

_____.

13. If my best friend were an animal, he or she would be a _____.

14. My best friend's favorite book is

_____.

15. My best friend has a crush on

_____.

16. The one thing I should never say to my best friend is _____.

How Well Does My Best Friend Know Me?

1. My best friend's birthday is _____ .

2. Circle the number of brothers and sisters your best friend has:

      a. 0   b. 1   c. 2   d. 3   e. 4   f. 5 or more

3. My best friend's favorite movie of all time is

   _____ .

4. My best friend's favorite movie star is

   _____ .

5. My best friend's favorite TV show is

   _____ .

6. My best friend's favorite music group is

   _____ .

7. The one food I should never serve to my best friend is

   _____ .

8. My best friend's favorite ice cream flavor is

   _____ .

KEROPPI'S SECRET CODE

9. My best friend's favorite subject in school is

   _____ .

10. My best friend's hobby is

    _____ .

11. My best friend's favorite sports team is

    _____ .

12. The thing my best friend likes to shop for most is

    _____ .

13. If my best friend were an animal, he or she would
    be a _____ .

14. My best friend's favorite book is

    _____ .

15. My best friend has a crush on

    _____ .

16. The one thing I should never say to my best friend
    is _____ .

CHeCK tHe NeXt page to FiND oUt
HoW WeLL yoU ScoreD!

KERoPPI'S SECRET CoDE

How Well Did You Score?

- **New Friends:** 0–3 questions right. Did you two just meet this morning? You really need to get to know each other better. But at least you're off to a good start!

- **Just Pals:** 4–7 questions right. Not bad, but you might want to hang out together a little more. Take a walk! Go see a movie! This friendship is worth it.

- **Best Buddies:** 8–12 questions right. You two are always there for each other. But there still might be some secrets about each other that you don't know. . . .

- **Fast Friends:** 13–15 questions right. You two are perfect for each other. I bet people think you are related!

- **Friends Forever:** 16 questions right. Congratulations! If there were a Friendship Hall of Fame, you two would be in it!

Low score? Don't worry! Try taking the quiz again in a few weeks and see how you do.

KEROPPI'S SECRET CODE

It was great meeting you and your best friend! I hope the two of you have lots of fun together. Before you go, here's the answer to my secret message:

Good-bye!

You finished this book so fast! I'm still on page 1.

Roses are red,
Violets are blue.
Remember this message
From me to you.

A best friend
is always there for you,
Whether you're happy
or just feeling blue.

So be good to your
best friend
Whatever you do.
Remember this message
From Keroppi to you!